Rush

Of

Many

Waters

Also by Pauly Hart

Rush of Many Waters:
Volume Eleven
By Pauly Hart

Contents

Terminus H

The hub system was a middle red hub on the inside with six hubs on the outside. Everything was very professional.

We all travelled there in a desert skimmer and docked at the dock hub.

We all proceeded at a leisurely pace, ready for the seminar. This would be the largest amount of people ever at the terminus.

There was a man who had come with us, who had been very impatient to board and unboard the skimmer. There were no first class seats so he had to sit in the middle. His carry-on was on 8 casters and was box shaped. "Porta-forms Inc." was written on the side in a heavy white font.

When we arrived, there was no pushing or shoving but he was very insistent and politely demanding. He 'needed to get off very quickly' was all he would say, almost illegally.

He had on a mustard yellow shirt and had very thin sandy brown hair and seemed happy when he was finally unboarded. I will never forget the brief moment in time where our arm hairs brushed against one another, for this would be the shortest moment in time where I would be next to but not part of the entire heist.

He walked a bit more quickly than casual, which was rude but not against the law. Out here, you really didn't have any law, but we all regarded the common Calilaw all the same. Law said that you couldn't do that, but there he was, inching past us, a stride longer. By the time the rest of us got to the door of the main Terminus, he was moving towards the doorway already setting up his box.

He had been hunched over while he was walking, pushing a rod here, moving a bar there, and installing his small black device as he rolled it along. It was a very strange thing to do, and quite possibly against many Calilaw social customs, but there he was doing it. So that, by the time he was at the door to the middle hub, the black bottom slid right over the threshold of the door.

The terminus, all being mostly hexagonal in nature, fit together in such a way where the doors that connected each one were a little off to the side of where you would expect them to be. So when we rounded the last right corner to the main hub, there was still a bit of a turn to get to the door around the connecting wall.

The device was like the underbelly of a large roach. The bottom wheels snapped outward as the side-poles telescoped up to find the head jab. They locked in place, and from the bottom, what looked like venetian blinds in reverse slicked up the middle. It rolled up fairly quickly as well – like an old fashioned garage door. When we rounded the corner, much to our surprise, in the few steps it took to get there, he had already effectively sealed himself inside of it. I remember seeing his eyes. They were a dead yellow.

This was a crisis. No one knows what to do in a crisis. No one trains for a crisis. We all stood there for a moment, not knowing what to do or say. The woman standing next to me, in a large orange summer dress said something about 'waiting until they open it' but she it was nervous-chat she just needed to have something to say.

Soon, a steward appeared and told us that refreshments would serve refreshments in one of the antechamber hubs. For the most part, the people left, milling about the entrance, with furtive glances over their shoulders at the major dilemma in the middle of the Terminus foyer. A short man with close-cropped black hair and glass-frames and I were soon the only ones left.

He said something about the "normals not knowing how to take assertive when they saw the need for it" and I readily agreed. I had been sizing up the framework around the joints to the door. His black box had been designed by the same company as the entire Terminus, so when he had sealed himself in the scaly black man-trap he had done so in a perfect location. There, at the floor, the feet of his device had slid in with ease to the floor seams. So his structure fit into the pre-existing structure like it had meant to go there.

Porta forms knew what they were all about and this was a class fit. The Terminus itself consisted of many portable units, that was their appeal. Instant shelter wherever. Out here in the Coachella Valley, near the Salton Sea, it was a perfect solution. But with the intruder's new addition, it also served as a complete barricade against anyone moving around it.

There was only one window on each of the walls of the terminus and I walked over to it to see what was transpiring inside. The programmers all sat at their desks, watching the man in the mustard shirt giving a practiced speech over a speaker. He had what looked like an old PDA (or a mobile phone) in his left hand and in his right he was pointing to the front holo-board. He seemed a little manic and waved his hand periodically, as if to prove a point. The programmers seemed a little amused, but laughed at him. This would probably be the most excitement of their lives. They weren't even aware that they were hostages.

Soon, the alarms were ringing. A soft yellow blip from the ceiling and a holo showing a man in a uniform smiling and asking people to 'remain calm' with a pleasant Kiwi voice. He repeated it in several languages. There was no security here. Middle-tech had not planned for anything like this. Probably the police from El Centro had been called and they were mobilizing at this very moment. I wondered what would their response time be.

While I had been studying the situation, I had downloaded the Porta-forms blueprints for the Terminus as well as the "Scufflewall 5200" – The device the man in the mustard shirt was inside of. It had been a special order from the Mumbai Police fifteen years ago, but somehow, he had access to one. His was all Pseudo-plas so I would not be able to break it.

At the top lip of the joints of the terminus, there was a fold-over of the composite metal to the Pseudo-plas. Only a centimeter or so, for pressure purposes or instability in the footing, and there was a foam gasket underneath it to match the seal. I said something to the small man about "doing the only thing I was trained to do" – lifted up and pinched my fingers at the top seam.

My estimations were at the thickness of the composite metal, they had not been included in the blueprints. By overestimating, I would need 15.42 tons per foot of pressure to bend the lip down. So, with my right fingers secure on the top lip, I placed my right leg on the wall to the right. Then I telescoped out my left arm to behind my back and then placed my left leg on the wall as well and then pulled downward and to the left. This brought a low wrenching sound to the ears and some excitement on the inside of the Terminus. The man in mustard said something to the tune of "nothing can happen now because the damage was already done".

I readjusted and pulled again, this time, peeling the wall more than half a meter down. When I pulled a third time, the wall bent down to the ground and I straightened myself and walked thru.

The faces of the people were not alarmed as you would see most normals, but placid and bored. I stepped by their desks and approached the man in the mustard shirt. With a "passcodes are changed, data is downloaded, nothing here is valuable anymore" he gave me his device. It was indeed an old mobile... What they used to call a phablet. I regarded it and tucked it into my jacket. The man smiled. I told him the authorities were on the way. He laughed and told me that he was one of the authorities.

The small man with glass frames agreed. This was a Homeland Security raid. All of the programmers around us were criminals and we had just saved a hostile takeover in Malaysia.

This was crime now. As an android, I never thought I would live to see the day. Humans used to be... Less boring.

Odd Minds

Fulerton clicked into his mind, the quickest movements and the largest guesses. He knew the circles were inside of circles. He had built the machine anyway. Poles and gears and pulleys and winches were just a thing made of man, not a magical force. There was Astro William with his banjo, the man who reminded him of Data from Star Trek; then there was the giant as well. The only thing fitting him was that awful yellow sun-dress.

If he could get them both out, it would be a miracle. Just then he ran left. The burned out house shifted with the machine and threatened to close him off. Dust spilled as the door was lifted into the air. Enormous shafts thrust up, breaking through the rubble. The giant had been leaning back against a concrete slab and was thrown off balance.

It was a gear within a gear within a gear. He clicked his mind over and saw how this newest circle moved and gave way to the next. All the circles connecting together, all at once. Three gears later and he had the whole thing configured. He jogged a little forward and then pointed almost directly behind him as an old Buick lurched and moved with the slope of the ground shifting.

"There!" Fulerton shouted. "Follow me!"

Both Astro William and the giant were weaving in and out of building debris, right behind him. The ground moved up and then down as the building swayed towards them, almost buckling. Another pole shot up from the ground, this one was about the size of a soda can, and continued up towards the ceiling.

"Machine getting ready to make new machine!" The giant yelled, his large voice almost muffled by the collapse of another wall.

Fulerton wondered if he was right. He ducked into a doorway, glancing to make sure the others were still behind him. It was hard to see but they were there, hot on his trail. He went forward, a little left. This building had not begun to move but that didn't mean the gears were heading that direction. In the room was a back door and a side door. He moved to the side door, this part of the puzzle not being clear. It was better to go left than forward.

As the door opened he heard a large click and instantly regretted it. There was the beginning of the maze – perfectly calm. No dust, no broken tables, walls intact. The back door was the solution, but it was no use now. If he opened it now it would just be part of this new maze, the old exit closed to him.

He walked in and sat down. Fulerton and the giant came in after. "What now?" Astro William asked, setting his banjo down.

"We try again." Fulerton said.

"I'm hungry" said the giant.

She held her snifter in the direction it should go and pulled from the reaches of her brain. It wasn't an actual north, but a direction that the snifter chose. Whatever she needed would be able to be traced to that spot... But she was chasing Carl and he had done his disappearing trick again. Wasn't it days ago that they had shared that little tent? It was so small, but they had taken away their "ready-room" and forced them all to get to know each other.

He held up the ping pong ball she had thrown at him. The end was cut off and it was red like a clown nose. Cute. There were three of them. He couldn't tell which one had thrown it. Old Tom had been talking to him, and Dave was still wandering around, seeing old friends. He was waiting on his "Diet Wendy" whatever that was. He was thinking of ordering a Cherry Tab himself – which was weird. No one had Tab anymore. These guys did. He held up both balls towards the girls. They smiled and did that little shoulder swivel/butt shake that horny girls do. They were playing some sort of beer-pong for kids with a digital score-card. The machine looked like an old air-hockey table.

"Here. You should wear this as a nose, cause you throw like a clown." He said because it was the most obvious thing to say.

"Don cha wanna play wit us?" the leader of the girls cajoled.

They had to be around eighteen or nineteen. The leader had a large scar on her face. Maybe younger, maybe older. He had no idea how old they were, but here they were all the same. Until they exploded and he caught on fire. He was going to die, and so much had been left undone.

With a lurch, she sat up and began to tear off the electrodes glued to her head. The large gray gargoyle lay beside her, a thin pink sweat trickling off its brow.

Jason, back in the sub-control room, asked her: "Everything alright?"

"I'm fine." she said. "We were derailed by sex... And clowns." She pursed her lips, shaking her head.

"Clowns?" Jason asked. "There were clowns?"

"Just a nose." she said, "but it's a sign that he knows something isn't right. I've never seen clowns before."

"Clowns are bad then, I'll write that down." Jason said.

"It was a red clown nose." she said. "Not really a clown." she said.

"Gotcha." Jason said. "Power cycle?"

"Yup." she agreed.

She got off the table and walked around to the main control. She closed the program and turned to the large computer behind her. She hit the "Power cycle" button and watched the lights blink and the engine whir. The whole room dissolved as did her clothes, her hands, and her feet. Back to the void. Dream mechanics were a horrible business, but Victor was still asleep so she would try to get into his mind again and this time, get to his root brain. Jason agreed.

With a lurch, she sat up, and began to take the helmet off her head. Alex, back in the sub-control room asked her: "Everything alright?"

"Yeah." she said. "Check Jason's notes. It should have everything there."

"Coming in now." Alex said. "Power cycle?"

"No. I think we're far enough out to try again from here." she said. She looked over at the black Yeti. His left arm had fallen on the floor. That was odd.

"How long has this instantiation had only three limbs?"

"Um…" Alex said.

With a lurch, she sat up, and began to take off her head.

Upper Stratosphere

The Labract Spectre Unit had been interviewing methane particles in the stratosphere when the ship first entered the atmosphere. Actually it was more a trail of debris and pluming steam than a recognizable form. The ship careened into the burn-zone of the Troposphere with the inertia of a small moon. Labract Spectre Unit #BRAZI4IXA was swept up in the turbulence...

>>>>Gimbal: Negative Control<<<<

>>>>Altitude: Negative Control<<<<

>>>>Gyros: Negative Control<<<<

Great. Brazi4xia was now careening also. In a flat spin and falling at 525 Kru. Pull up! He was now enveloped in the cloud of black smoke and steam that the falling ship had left behind. Out of control and spinning in this way, he realized that there was more to the fall than just the backwash. He should have been able to break free by now. But the controls were not responding... What was the problem?

>>>>Iridium Depleted<<<<

>>>>Statofield Depleted<<<<

>>>>Magnetosphere Depleted<<<<

Of course! The falling ship had come out of Flux! That would explain why most of his controls were still gone. He knew that this relatively new part of earth kept in orbit several Proximity Unjoiners for flux drives that were coming too close to the project. But this ship had come out of Flux a broken wreckage... their Flux Drive was corrupted and the coil was giving out a broad Electromagnetic Wave that was discharging everything in its path. There would be no chance of regaining flight unless he broke free of the magnetic jet stream that the ship was leaving behind. But what else could he do?

He checked his Altimeter control.

>>>>Altimeter: Control Negative<<<<

"How uninspiring. I should have a much more glorious death than this one." he thought... He looked "up" and saw the ground looming towards him at a speedy rate. In 157 seconds or less he would become nothing more than a small dent in that dirt himself. What could he do?

Nothing but watch.

Commander Yoq in the Morning

Chief Security Commander of Squadron One, Inio Alephandri Yoq, climbed down to the ground from Recon 5. The Security Ship held up to twenty passengers or ten security robots, depending. Today it was her and the top nine of her Damram.

Her mission: Find out what the hell happened at the Mephisto. So basically: Capture suspects. Kill renegades. Bring in witnesses. Control the media. Clean up. She suspected that this would be nothing more than a mop-up job at best, with no real leads to show from it.

The media had ceased yapping about gangs; it actually scared them to pieces. No one wants to hear about a bunch of crazy kids with guns blowing each other away. Not sponsors anyway. Oh hell, she didn't want to hear about it either. But here she was, and there was work to be done. But it pissed her off all the same.

Those stupid gang members. That's all I need now. First Lo-Ami takes out the Neo-Sushi on live TV, and now I have to deal with this! Commander Yoq was New Boston's top officer. She took down the entire Kidd gang by herself. Any cop who had a record like that could get whatever they wanted. But all she wanted was to kick some ass... And that was fine with her authorities. However, the cops these days weren't as tough as her. The numbers of actual humans in the COPCORP was dropping with each year.

There were some problems with that, but it meant that the competition for choosing assignments was slim to none. And that, she had no problem with. "Alright boys. Search out the Mephisto. I want my best two with me. Sgt. Goraw, I want you and the rest of the Damram to search out the alleyways. I'm going to take a look inside."

Sgt. Goraw nodded and with a mechanical voice said, "Move out." Human cops weren't that efficient these days... With all the gangs running around they didn't have enough stamina to catch up with them. But Damram on the other hand? They were the key to keeping this city in peace; they didn't need to eat or sleep, just some repairs and some go-juice and they were good to go. Actually, she had no idea what it took to run one of those beasts. They ran, and that was enough for her. Let the 'Docs worry about 'em. I'm just here to clean up. She looked at her nails and sighed. She hated getting her nails broken... especially when picking up stupid gang trash. She was better than this, she was better than all of them.

The two Damram units were like her shadows. They were programmed that way: Ernie and Bert. She had named them off some obscure 2-Vid she had seen many years ago. Wherever she turned... they turned. Whatever she fired at, they would also fire at. They were exact mimes of her. That is, until she released them on some preset program stored into their memory. Recon Program 4 Modification D effective now... And so forth...

Her green eye blinked and surveyed the dead outside with high band impacting. Her brown eye blinked as her iris focused on the Mephisto. The UV picked up no one alive inside. They're all gone. Great. Just corpses now. She should probably go check it out anyway. Hopping on Bert, they flew into the scene.

Sgt. Goraw didn't have much luck either. He scanned the perimeter and nothing showed in his visuals. "Move out. Nothing confirmed." The six Damram Units with him began to move when Damram Venture spoke.

"Sir! Visual confirmed, in sector 67-1! Scan concludes two DNA signs. One seems to be Feline! Possibly a mutation or something else undetermined. The other has a carbon base, but it seems metalloid, possibly robotic."

Sgt. Goraw flexed his LM-2 Tiger Style Prototype. He might try it out sooner than parameters had anticipated. "Belay first order. Proceed to 67-1. Assault Formation 1-A." The Damram all pulled their Pulse Rifles from out of their arms. "I will stay here and resume Com with the Commander. Now go!" Six deadly figures took off silently into the night sky, eyes gleaming a dark purple, Projacks glowing a silent red.

Sgt. Goraw's Com program clicked on and he spoke. "Commander Yoq. We have picked up two DNA sigs," He said.

She responded. "Good work Sgt. Goraw. I want them alive and well. Use the Slepurr packs on them. I want to see them zonked out like babies."

"Affirmative and out." Sgt. Goraw opened up her Com to Venture and the other Damram.

"Venture, start Capture Program 102, Commander Yoq's orders. I am coming to you as we speak. Do not engage until I arrive."

Venture responded, "Affirmative Sergeant. " Sgt. Goraw's torso seemed to bulge, and something like a third arm came out of his torso. But the thing was mobile, and seemed to crawl up his head until it covered both head and left shoulder. The Tiger Style Prototype warmed green and blinked.

"1010111001101100010001011010," it beeped. Sgt. Goraw beeped back to it: "Affirmative." His Projack pulsed and he was away.

Yoq jumped off the Damram and looked around. The faces of the Ghettogals gang looked so innocent, like ordinary girls, like orphans. Yoq's demeanor changed. They were whores. Street trash in pretty outfits. Thinking boys will want them because of their bodies. Thinking they were the queens of the night just because of their technology. Commander Yoq laughed. She used to be a member of this pathetic gang. Perhaps that's why she gave them such an easy time. She could have busted them so many times, but instead she just let them slide. Empathy? Yes, she guessed that's what it was. The Ghettogals had given her a chance to break out of the slums.

But that had been a lifetime ago. She sent Ernie and Bert to look in the club. She kicked around outside. Too many deaths. Too much pride in their little heads. They thought they were all that. They thought they could rule the world. But that's the problem... Each gang thought the exact same thing. Stupid sluts. I've seen their tags around town. Even on the Matrixnode. 'Angels of the Ghetto.' Yeah right. She kicked the glass away and sighed heavily. It was going to be a long day.

Poems

Luther's' Doxology

For thou, God, are from now until forever,
your mercies, they are new every morning.
And thou, God, encompass the earth with charity.
Thy loving kindness is new every morning.

Come Lord Jesus, be our guest this eve.
And let thy gifts to us be blessed, we pray thee.
For thine is the kingdom, and the glory, and the power.
Thy loving kindness is made new in the morn.

The Lord encompasses the Earth with much grace.
And His blood doth flow, blotting out mine sin.
Oh give thanks unto the Lord for He is good.
And His mercies endures forever.

Amen.

Door

The things that you say to me
I have heard many times before
From countless lovers girl
As they're walking out the door

But I know there's a difference
Between my love and yours
Your love is the ocean
And I am the moon
I said your love is the ocean

And I am - the moon

The unfathomable chasm
From your heart to your mind
Cannot begin to love me
Cannot begin to find

That there is a vast difference
Between my love and yours
For Your love is the ocean
And I am the moon
I said your love is the ocean
And I am - the moon

I walked, I have seen
I talked, believed
In something like you
I have seen someone like you
Oh just like you
In my dreams

The things that you say to me
I have heard many times before
From countless lovers girl
As they're walking out the door

But I know there's a difference
Between my love and yours
Your love is the ocean
And I am the moon
I said your love is the ocean
And I am - the moon

Task of the leader
(inspired by Dick Foust
and the pain of his leadership)

Hire people smarter than you are
Find out your talents inside
Loving makes you look better
Surround yourself with free thinkers
Fear will destroy all you've worked for
Envy will destroy your company
Is it your company or Gods anyway
Encourage employees to exceed you
Don't limit your staffs imagination
Fire all of your "Yes" men
Admit your failures readily
Be a touchable and reachable person
Ask for constructive criticism
And take it like a man
Listen and understand, don't assume
Delegate responsibility don't dump
Don't use people, let them feel useable
Trust and be secure in your work force

You know, it's amazing what
can be accomplished, when you
never worry about who gets the credit

Public Domain

Grey/Gray

I'm lost in a world of gray.
when you stand nowhere today.
forever is like the tide.
it's waves bend us in our minds.

i need you more than the state.
did you know i cannot hate?

i'm lost in a world of gray.
when you stand so far away.

Relax

If everyone felt relaxation
coming out of their nose
If everyone felt
the feeling coming
out

out

of their noses
choking on happiness
until they died of hope
If they knew life
then they would die

Go for it

When life seems to drag you down

And life's problems make you drown

Then you should always look around

And go for it

In its simple, simple way

Questions never do obey

So you look around and say

"I'll go for it."

When life's decisions pass you by

And all time does is fly

Don't you fret and don't you cry

Just go for it

And when seeing is not believing

You go for it

                                        It's ok

I feel hated, I feel used, I am angry, I am abused
It's ok, this feeling that's deep down inside
It's my anger that's reaching inside of my life

I feel cheated, abandoned, circling unlanded
I am fine in here, but not with her
It's my anger prickling like an angry cur

I feel disjointed, unloved from below to above
It's alright to be angry, I duly confess
I feel it all over, this hate I address

I feel and am pissed off about being thrown off
It is really unfair and it won't go away
I can't shake it, run or push it away

I feel angry and I know it ain't dandy
I feel angry, am seething inside my cage
I let it all go, my blame and my rage

It's ok to be angry, It's ok to feel pain
It's ok to be wrong, It's ok to take blame

hope for my own girlfriend

I heard the day breaking
I listened with heart attuned
I did take that view
And I did pursue
And if I am confused
I listen with ears of flesh

I feel the ocean swelling
Can I take you near the waves?
Why do you refuse
People you can't choose
Don't you feel so used
I watch you sink in the tide

When you smile you make my day
When you cast all the shadows away
And dark spills out crud
Covering my blood in mud
Have you been that low?
When the dawn breaks with Jesus's face

Failure

You failed my tired spirit
You failed

Like a bitch in heat you cry
You lied
Like a dripping faucet annoying
I tried
Like a maddened axe man throwing
I tried
Like blind conductors call
You suck
Every fiber in my soul it seems
You failed
You failed me
If I tried way too hard
Than it is not my fault

Childhood

A flower died
- I cried

I remember tricycles
- Spinning

They came and went
- And I sat

I wanted a friend
- Just one

But no one ever came
– For me

Poison Ivy

As the scream of terror wracks my convulsing body, I suddenly realize that all my efforts have been in vain to find the quiet resting spot of glory. I find that no matter how hard I try, I can never overcome the wanton disabilities of my writhing soul. I can never shake these diseased limbs to life. As I mop the chilly sweat from my brow, I realize my wrong.

Poison Ivy.

Spontaneous Psalm #14

Father I miss you
In my life today
And pray for those along the way
That have hurt me
Father I miss them in my life today
Though I can't have the opportunity to forgive them

Not really but... You know...
Hey, why not? Let's pray for our enemies!

Father touch my enemies
Those who hate me
Cure their sin
With something true

Oh Lord Jesus Christ
I forgive my mommy and my daddy
When I was a little kid
And I felt so abused
And all those things that
I thought they did
Or maybe I just took it wrong
Cause I didn't understand
Cause I was only three
Lord Jesus forgive them
Oh Father I please ask forgiveness

For the things I did
When I was seven
And then when I was eleven
And when I was twelve
And fifteen and seventeen
And twenty two
Father take all my
Blame and shame and crime away
Cause I don't want to have any
Grime before you
Lord I want to be clean
Want to be holy
Want to be pure
Want to be spotless
Want to be wrinkle free
Wash me in the tide
That is alright
That is cool and breezy
With you
Oh shoot me down and
Wash me clean
And scrub me
Scrub me scrub me do
Cause I wanna be clean for you
Oh touch me Jesus
Take my sin
Lord don't let it stink again
Cause it stank a long, long time
And I'm so sick of the grime
And the crime and I just wanna
Praise you with it
Give it to you
Take all my sin
And throw it at the foot of the cross
Cause I know that's where
It belongs anyway
And now Jesus
Oh Jesus, Jesus

Touch me now
Touch me Lord
Touch my head
Touch my cap
Touch my gown
And I thus pray
Lord touch me now
Lord touch everything that I have
And everything that I pray for
Lord I pray for the prayers of my life
I pray for the intercessors
Those who would lift me up to you
Jesus I thank you Lord God
For everybody whose touched my life
And I just pray
That my tires would stay round
That my head would stay tan and brown
And Lord I just ask that
I don't know
I don't even have a tan
What am I sayin… I'm a white man
You know what I'm sayin Lord God
But I don't care
You made me this color
And I don't care Lord Jesus
I wanna praise you
With everything that I've got
Everything that I'm not
I just want to give to you because
Lord I just want to give you all
I give you everything
That's why my name is Paul, Lord

I give you everything that I have

I give that I have to you
Everything that's not pink and blue
Oh sure, Lord you can have that too

Cause they're only arbitrary colors before you

What do you know man
You know everything
I don't know anything man
You're just so big and holy
And so pure and spotless
And I'm just a little kid
Man I think I know it all
And I've only been here
What? a couple of years
And you've been there a zillion
Wait a minute…
You created time
How could you have even
Been there a zillion

A zillions like a second
Lord let me worship you for a second then

Yeah and times three nine nine
Woah and just a second to you
Is but a zillion years to us humans
Sure am glad you came and
Went thru it with us
So you could know what it was all about

Yeah yeah yeah
Give everything that I have to you
Jesus worshipping you is everything that I wanna do
I don't want to do anything else Lord
Food doesn't seem important any more man

Essays

Yeah, right.

The greatest miracle that this world ever saw was not when Jesus came to the earth as a human. No, the greatest miracle as well as the greatest act of faith began when Christ was killed and died. For it was at this miracle beginning time that several things happened at once.

First of all, Christ, or, God-made-flesh, had died. A seemingly unexpected and unprepared-for act of the greatest importance. It is debated whether God-made-flesh descended into Hell and wrestled with Lucifer for the Keys to Death and the grave, or whether he went to Abraham bosom, and showed himself to them, giving the first rapture. He could have died Spiritually. No one but God knows for sure.

Second of all, The Father, or Jehovah, had rejected a part of himself. Because Christ had taken all sin, sickness, disease, and poverty upon himself at the cross, Father could no longer look upon him. He turned his back and allowed his favor to lift. Hence, causing the greatest separation since the first, in the garden.

Thirdly, The Spirit, or the Comforter, left the ark of the Covenant. For centuries, since the time of Moses, He had dwelled in this Ark. Inside of tabernacles, and several different temples, He had resided with His people. But now, with the curtain tore in two, He apparently turned His back on Christ as well.

Fourthly, all of Hades, Hell, Sheol, Abbadon, Gehena, Tardes, Death, and the Grave rejoiced. Not to mention the Fallen Angels, Principalities, Powers, Rulers, Nephilim, Demons, Devils, Foul Spirits, The Strongman, Beelzebub, and especially the Great Deceiver himself; had one Hell of a party.

But I really think that the greatest thing, the single act of sheer obedience to bring the world to attention was the fact that Christ trusted The Father to bring Him back from the dead. He preached and healed in faith, He lived in faith, He was taken before court in faith, He was beaten in faith, and He was ripped and shredded in faith. Faith that the Father would be true to His word. Faith that the joy set before Him would become a reality. Think about it. Without that one holy act of faith, Christ may never have died. He had the power not to didn't He? He might still be alive today. But He had to. But without that act of total obedience, and without the sovereign act of the Father, Jesus might still be in Hell today.

Yeah right, like that could ever happen.

The wise sayings of Ratuna Fonsaire

The only difference between a big ass and a healthy butt is about 24 inches

I want to be the leader of all of the anarchists

If I was a teen superstar and I was featured in Teen-Beat Magazine, I would be very ashamed if people put a poster of me on their wall.

If it were up to me: Heavy set, unibrowed Italian mafia types wouldn't be allowed to wear thick gold necklaces, cause it might get caught in their chest-hair... And we should really be nice to people like that.

I've often wondered about the secret life of Bruce Willis. The guy makes a lot of money and then goes around doing cameos in shitty movies. I mean, if I were a famous actor and had money out the wazoo then would I make shitty movie appearances? I don't know, perhaps the life of the famous and wealthy is too challenging to sit at home all of the time. Maybe he cameos in movies that suck just so people won't forget him. Uh, you know, that one guy.

Doesn't it bug you when people smoke? I mean, like: Hey! That's $4.25 that you could be spending on MY bad habits!

I think that if I were a black cat I would spend all day on fence-posts and just look cute but then go "Rarrrw!" every time someone came near me to pet me... Or maybe if I was an indoors dog and it was like 3:30 in the morning I would bark and wake everyone up and when they came to see what was the matter I would stand in front of the basement door and just growl, and then when my master came back with a baseball bat I would just wag my tail and trot away and be like: WHAT???

If I was a girl I would get a tattoo on my bikini line that said: "I want to fuck steve" cause then when every guy got to third base with me they would be like: "Hey! Who's Steve?"

You know... What's with bears? They're big, ugly, smell terrible and eat people! So why did my mother make mw sleep with them as a child?

I love women who love sex, cause then you can get them all horny and then dump them, cause who wants that?

I often wonder why the sky is blue and then I think - Oh it's because of certain wavelengths in our color spectrum are reflected out of the Earths Ionosphere and then I light up a smoke cause that's just messed up.

I love looking down into the toilet at my dump before I wipe, cause it's really cool to just see it sitting there all helpless, forlorn, and alone... and wiggly. But then I notice that it's a big tapeworm and it makes me mad because: "Hey that's MY lunch".

Goodbye

Goodbye to sprinkler parks, slide parks and dinosaur books. To Barbie houses and Underoos. Goodbye to School schedules and goodnight kisses. Goodbye to making toast and cleaning up under the table. Goodbye to sticky fingers.

Goodbye to distracting smells that erupt out of nowhere. Goodbye to car seats and finding bugs in the back yard. Goodbye to favorite cups, spoons and reading before bed-time. Goodbye to front-back-middle, and to e-sa-no. Goodbye Angel Wars and Legos.

Goodbye to hair messes, shampoo, training seats, step stools. Goodbye to all of that.

Goodbye to the future of us. Goodbye to the feeling embarrassed when I acted silly around you. Goodbye to terrible sex, to your stifled dried-up emotions, and goodbye to typo corrections. Goodbye to your picky pet peeves and to your horrible singing voice. Goodbye to your credibility stamp on my issues that I dealt with. Goodbye to being measured up against every day.

Goodbye to the confidence and satisfaction I felt as "your mate". Goodbye to your free schooling and the potential that life was finally showing us. Goodbye for not being invited into your heart. For not being welcome to your grand-dads funeral. Goodbye to the showers I took while you watched. Goodbye to your stinky times of the month.

Goodbye to the honeymoon we never had, goodbye to "your" money. To your opinion of my writings, goodbye to "As soon as we" promises. Goodbye to that special someone I could always look to for a sarcastic remark, and to snub me when I helped her. Goodbye to my other half. Goodbye to that person who shared my bed. Goodbye to you. Goodbye to pain.

Goodbye lack of appreciation... that never a "thank you" mouth. Goodbye to your calloused sensitivity. Goodbye to the approval I so needed from you. Goodbye to your silly little video games, goodbye to your warped sense of Gods justice, to your lies, to your controlling attitude. Goodbye to the fatal attraction I had for you.

Goodbye to you hair, your smells, your wardrobe. Goodbye to your bad heart, back, knees, head. Goodbye to your criticisms. Goodbye to sarcasm at it's finest. Goodbye to the immature baby who runs to mama every time she almost gets something accomplished. Goodbye to the name calling and to the unfaithful attitudes. Goodbye to the Jesus you think you know. Goodbye to your blame shifting and your unhealthy marital viewpoints. Goodbye to your chauvinism, and complaining.

Goodbye to your incredibly hostile attitude towards churches and ministers. Goodbye to being told I had all the responsibility of God Almighty, but was never given the respect. Goodbye to expected telepathy, and unfound accusations involving my extra marital sex life and hatred against my poor memory. Goodbye for being judged when I made Chili-Mac. Goodbye to being second place under the children. Goodbye to the lame excuses and to your flight or fight mentality. Goodbye to all of your creditors who wrote letter after letter.

Goodbye to uncared for feelings and all the things taken for granted. Goodbye to your half promises and your poor value judgments upon my character. Goodbye to your mind-trips about killing the children and to the freakish suicidal tendencies that you own. Goodbye to those "nice" things I did for me that you thought were for you. Goodbye to the comparisons between me and every other lover you ever had. Goodbye to feeling jealous of Jess or Rob or Jack. Goodbye to the expectations placed and promises made. Goodbye to all of the things you drug out of me and stole from my heart.

Goodbye to my spending my time, energy and money in your bottomless pit of neediness. Goodbye to the un-fulfillment I got when I looked into your eyes. Goodbye to your hiding yourself under your walls. Goodbye to your manipulative devices, your cheap thrills at agitating me. Goodbye to the pain, your anger, your angst. Goodbye to miserable, terrible you.

Hello happiness when I wake! Hello joy at each new day. Hello fulfillment in myself, hello life without chains. Hello peace in my room. Hello faithfulness in my heart. Hello hope of new beginnings. Hello future, Hello Jesus! Where have you been all this time?

Hello new day! Hello everyone I meet that doesn't cling. Hello to peace that passes all understanding, and to jellybeans eaten without sharing. Hello again to the music that I love and to the God I thought had left me.

Hello Lord! Hello new dawns and new friends who bring laughter. Hello new beds and my own problems to fix. Hello beginning again with no one blaming me but myself. Hello new life, success, peace and tranquility. Hello again pauly hart.

Hallelujah Praise Center

Jesus Is Alive Worship and Hallelujah Praise Center only had fifty people in the auditorium that Sunday morning and there I was with my purple hair and my "This is not a Fugazi T-shirt" T-shirt and my face piercings. The people were very welcoming but right behind their eyes was the horrified look of "Oh my goodness, we need to protect the children!" The pastor/farmer got up to preach and pretty much demanded that I stand up and tell everyone where I was from and what had brought me to such a low state that I would need to dye my hair purple. No he didn't really say it like that, but it felt like it. No matter, in three months, I would be on the stage with the "Worship Band" playing congas and shaking a tambourine.

I settled in, got a job managing a coffeeshop in the tiny downtown of yet another rural Indiana town, but this time I doubted that Jason would do me wrong like my first wife. And it was a regular afternoon in 1999, while I was walking my daily deposit to the bank that I happened upon my first truthers. They handed me a videocassette tape and told me to "Watch the whole thing brother." On it was Bill Still's *The Money Masters* and *Police State 2000* by Alex Jones. I did watch the whole thing. My new roommates called me crazy but I watched every single second. And then I watched The Money Masters two more times. That Alex guy was a bit over the top for me.

Now, I had "known" about a lot of this, but I couldn't put my finger on any of it. It was one of those things where, you knew you had seen some pretty suspicious things and then you hear a fact about it and you say to yourself: "Well that makes sense." And this was the beginning of my journey into (what some would say is) the darker side of the truth movement. It became all I really wanted to know about and I devoured everything I could on the subject of alternate news. I was still studying the Bible and so I think with the Bible in one hand and alternate media in the other, I started a whole new way of life. It was also about this time that I discovered Coast to Coast AM. And it was on Coast to Coast AM that I first heard something about The Flat Earth Society. I had to know more about that so I went digging and came up with a bunch of bible verses that supported the theory and then I met my second wife and everything stopped.

So of course there was 9/11 2001 which put a damper on everything around everyone in the USA. My second wife (who was my girlfriend at the moment) looked at me and decided to go get married. So, as building seven was falling, we said vows and got hitched. I don't think that relationship was off to a good start, and sure enough, ended pretty terribly… Almost as bad as my first one. But hey, we learn and grow and love is no exception. So… Wife #2 got a hair brained idea and decided to have us move to Tulsa so we could be closer to my family. It was a really awkward move and didn't end well for anyone… And then she left me. She came home one night, packed up her three children and left the next morning.

www.ingramcontent.com/pod-product-compliance
Lightning Source LLC
Chambersburg PA
CBHW030153200626
46812CB00016B/1821